CLOUDY ZOO

ADMIT ONE

CLOUDY ZOO

THIS IGLOO BOOK BELONGS TO...

D0337167

igloobooks

Published in 2022
First published in the UK by Igloo Books Ltd
An imprint of Igloo Books Ltd
Cottage Farm, NN6 0BJ, UK
Owned by Bonnier Books
Sveavägen 56, Stockholm, Sweden
www.igloobooks.com

Copyright © 2021 Igloo Books Ltd

1122 005
6 8 10 9 7 5
ISBN 978-1-80022-448-3

Written by Daisy Edwards
Illustrated by Lee Cosgrove

Designed by Justine Ablett
Edited by Daisy Edwards

Printed and manufactured in China

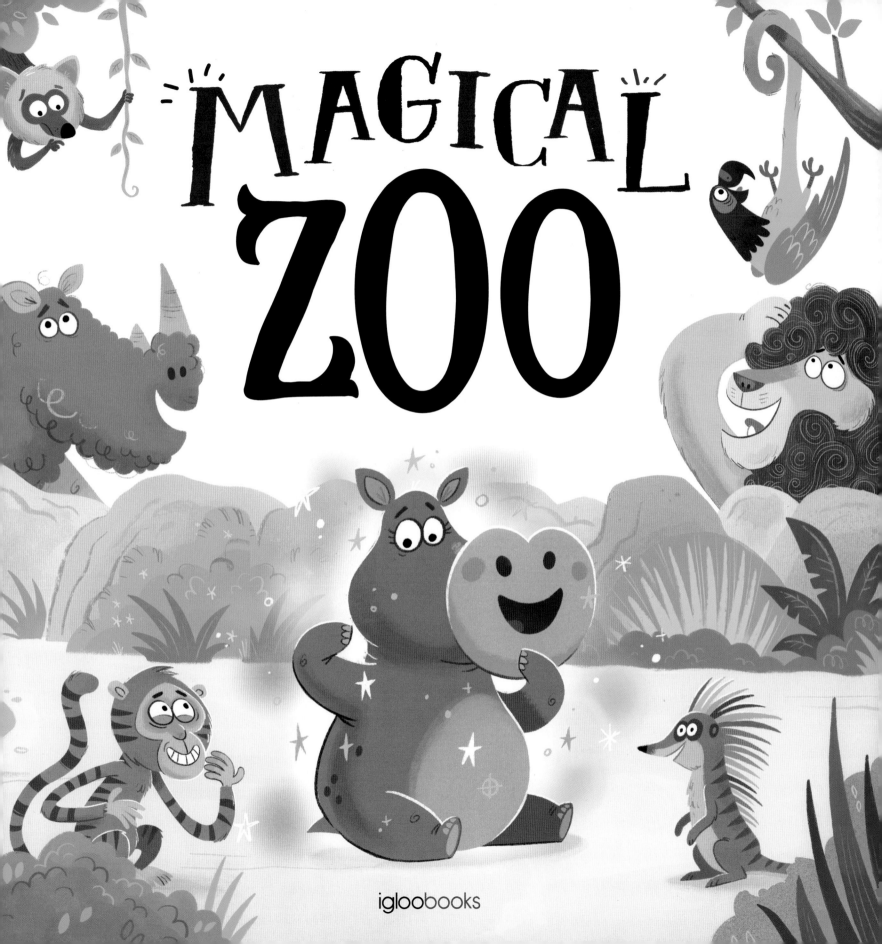

MAGICAL ZOO

igloobooks

There aren't any shows. Creatures don't make a sound.

When people walk in, they turn straight back around.

One night, Hippo hears a loud zookeeper say,

This zoo must close soon. It's so dull and grey!

Hippo makes a big wish,
when it starts getting late.

Please help save our zoo!
It could be so great.

When Hippo lies down for a sleep, with a yawn,

a creature appears. It's a cute...

FLUFFICORN!

She covers the zoo in a shimmery glow,
then floats off and smiles at the creatures below.

When the animals wake,
they know something has changed.

As they all look around,
what they see is so strange...

... Giraffe has a colourful, sparkly coat.
Rhino is fuzzy and Panda can float!

They all give their magical powers a try,
and Hippo shines bright as a star in the sky.

Giraffe shakes her fur,
with a dance and a wiggle...

... and Rhino does tricks
that make everyone giggle.